Wild Child

By Lynn Plourde

Illustrated by Greg Couch

Aladdin Paperbacks

New York London Toronto Sydney Singapore

First Aladdin Paperbacks edition September 2003

Text copyright © 1999 by Lynn Plourde
Illustrations copyright © 1999 by Greg Couch

ALADDIN PAPERBACKS
An imprint of Simon & Schuster Children's Publishing Division
1230 Avenue of the Americas, New York, NY 10020
Also available in a Simon & Schuster Books for Young Readers hardcover edition.
Designed by Paul Zakris
The text of this book was set in 22-point Lomba Medium.
Manufactured in China
10 9 8 7 6

The Library of Congress has cataloged the hardcover edition as follows:
    Plourde, Lynn.
        Wild child / Lynn Plourde ; illustrated by Greg Couch. —1st ed.
        p.   cm.
        Summary: Mother Earth attempts to put her wild child,
        Autumn, to bed.
        ISBN 0-689-81552-2 (hc)
        [1. Autumn—Fiction. 2. Seasons—Fiction. 3. Bedtime—Fiction.]
        I. Couch, Greg, ill. II. Title.
            PZ7.P724Wi 1999 [E]—dc21 98-15476   CIP   AC
            ISBN 0-689-86349-7 (pbk.)

A Note from the Artist:
I work on museum board; it's like a very thick, smooth watercolor paper. I put down many washes of liquid acrylic paint until I get the mood I'm looking for. Then, I add details for the faces, clothes, etc. with colored pencils. If the colors aren't bright enough after that I go back with a small brush and more acrylic to add the finishing touches.

With love to my own
wild child, Kylee
—L. P.

And with love to my
wild child, Emily
—G. C.

"Time for bed," Mother Earth said.
"Not for a while," said her wild child.
"A song, first.
I need a song
to play in my head
before going to bed."

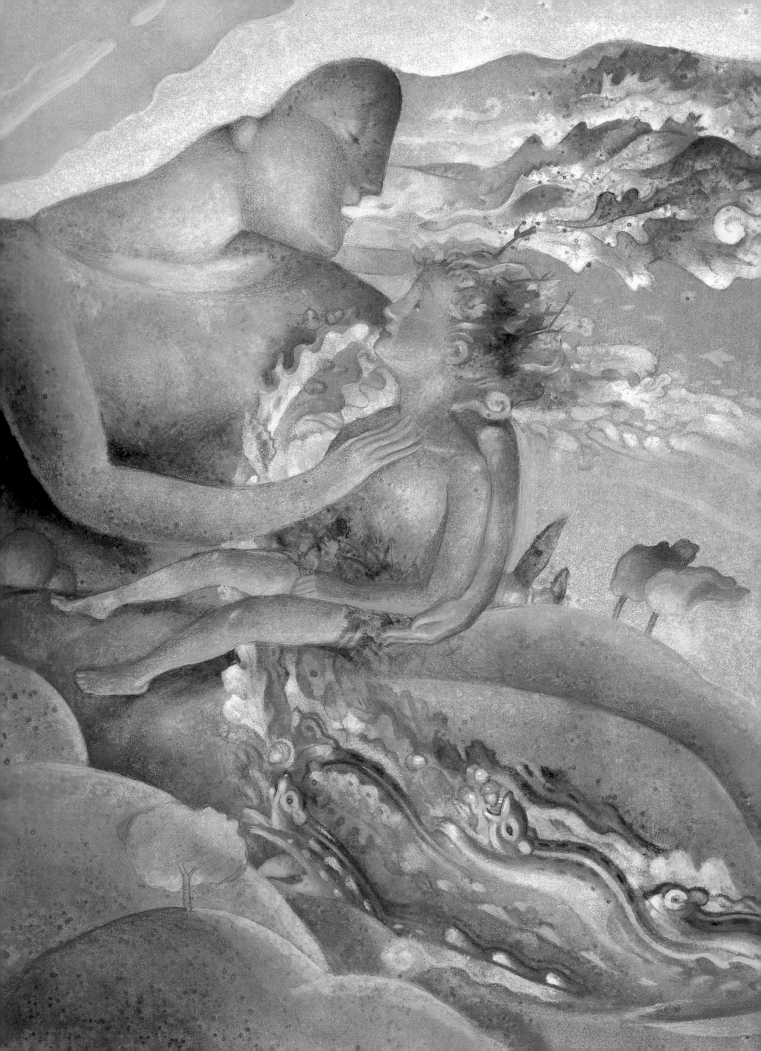

So Mother Earth
gave her child a song...

Crinkle, crackle,
leaves snapple.

Chutter, chatter,
chipmunks patter.

Flap, flitter,
birds twitter.

Skitter, scatter,
acorns splatter.

And such was the song
to play in her head.
And Mother Earth said,
"**NOW** are you ready for bed?"

"Not for a while," said her wild child.
"A bite, first.
I need a bite,
a little snack
before taking a nap."

So Mother Earth
gave her child a snack...

Crunchy, munchy,
chewy chestnuts.

Plumpy, lumpy,
pulpy pumpkins.

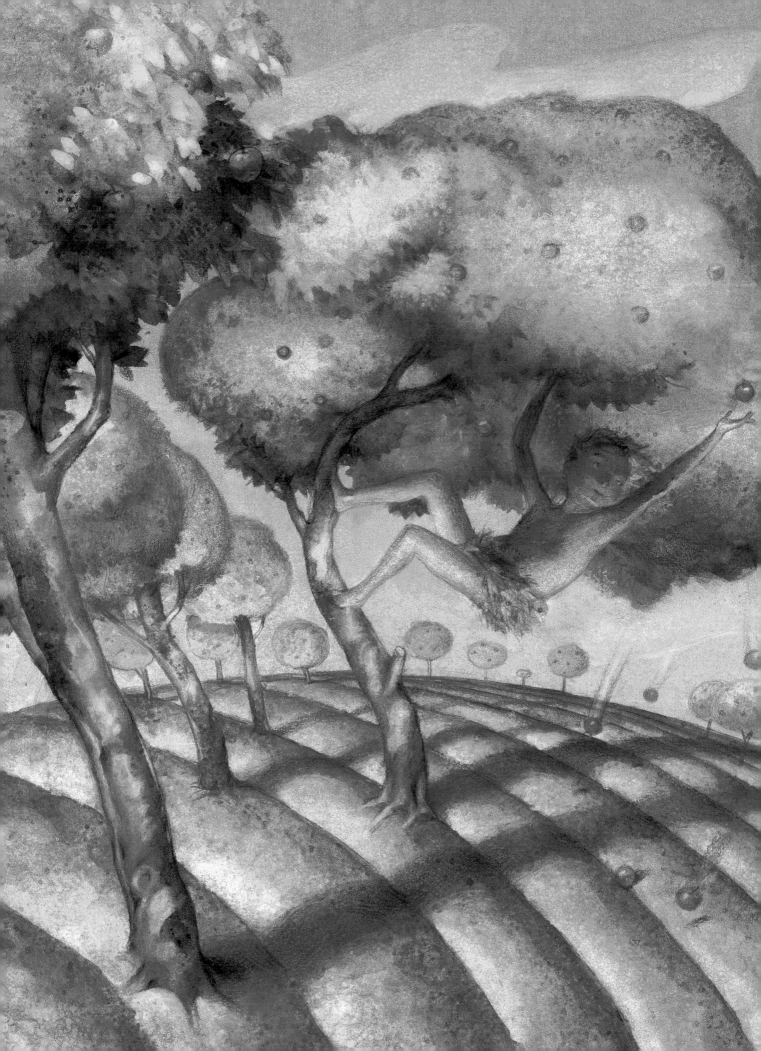

Snapperly, dapperly,
cidery apples.

Puckery, smuckery,
crimsony cranberries.

And such was the snack
before taking a nap.
And Mother Earth said,
"**NOW** are you ready for bed?"

"Not for a while," said her wild child.
"PJs, first.
I need PJs
to get all dressed
before taking a rest."

So Mother Earth
gave her child PJs...

A fiery, flaming,
reddish nightgown.

A brilliant, bursting,
yellowish robe.

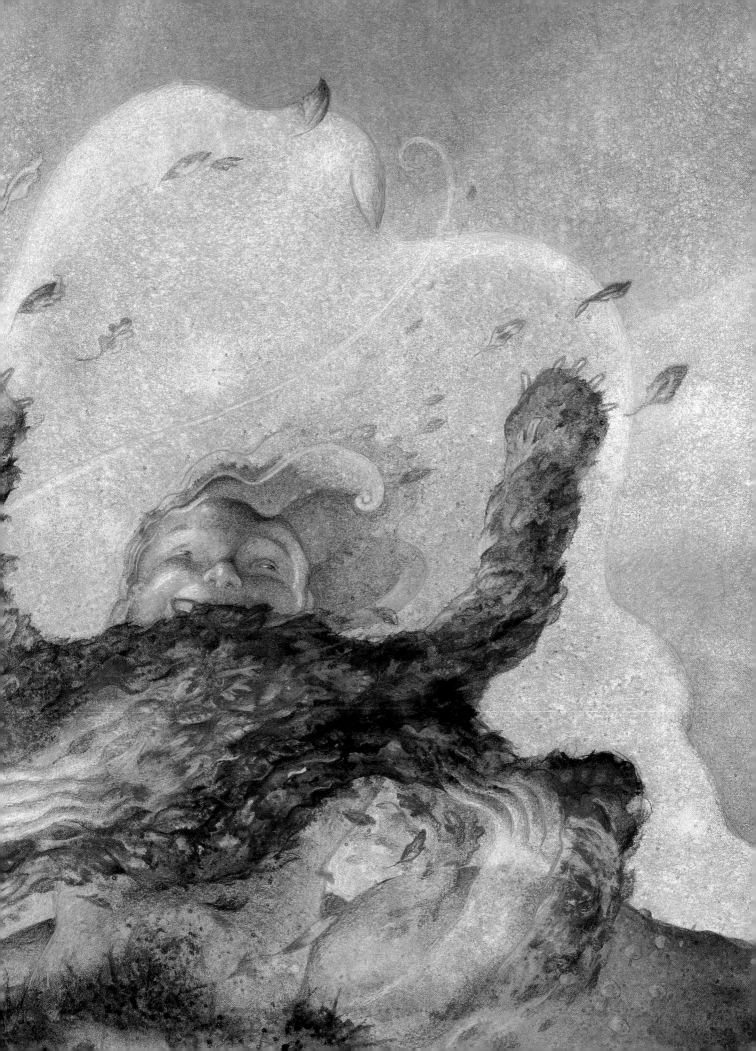

Two burnt, blistering,
orangish slippers.

A tawny, tarnished,
goldish nightcap.

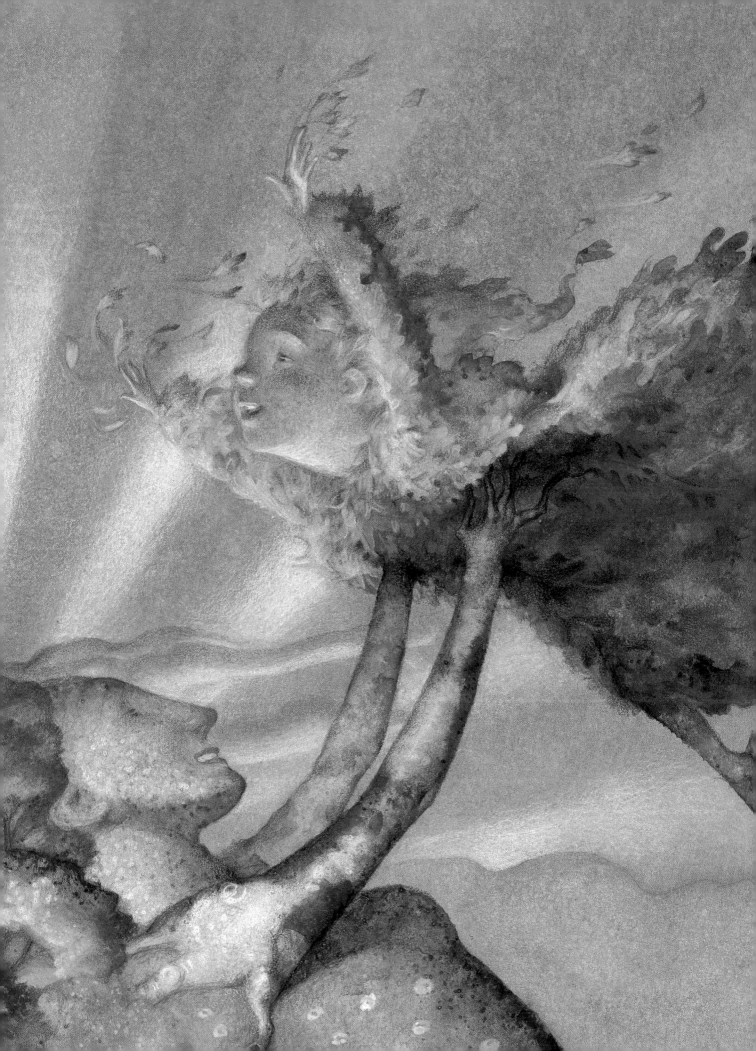

And that's how she was dressed
before taking a rest.
And Mother Earth said,
"**NOW** are you ready for bed?"

"Not for a while," said her wild child.
"A kiss, first.
I need a kiss,
a smooch and a smack
before hitting the sack."

So Mother Earth
gave her child a kiss...

A whooshy, whirlishy,
windswept snuggle.

A freezing, frizzling,
frosty caress.

A gusty, blustery,
twisty embrace.

A crystalish, icicle-ish,
icebergy kiss.

And such was the smooch and smack
before hitting the sack.

And Mother Earth proclaimed,
"Now you **ARE** ready for bed!"

This time her child smiled.
Yes, that wild child,

with a wink and a wiggle
and a stretch and a giggle,

hunkered below
a blanket of snow.

And let out a yawn
so loud and so long.

Her breaths grew deep
as she fell fast asleep.

And Mother Earth said,
while touching her head,
"Only sleep for a while,
for I shall miss my wild child,
my wild child called Autumn."

Then Mother Earth
put herself to bed,
finally resting her head.

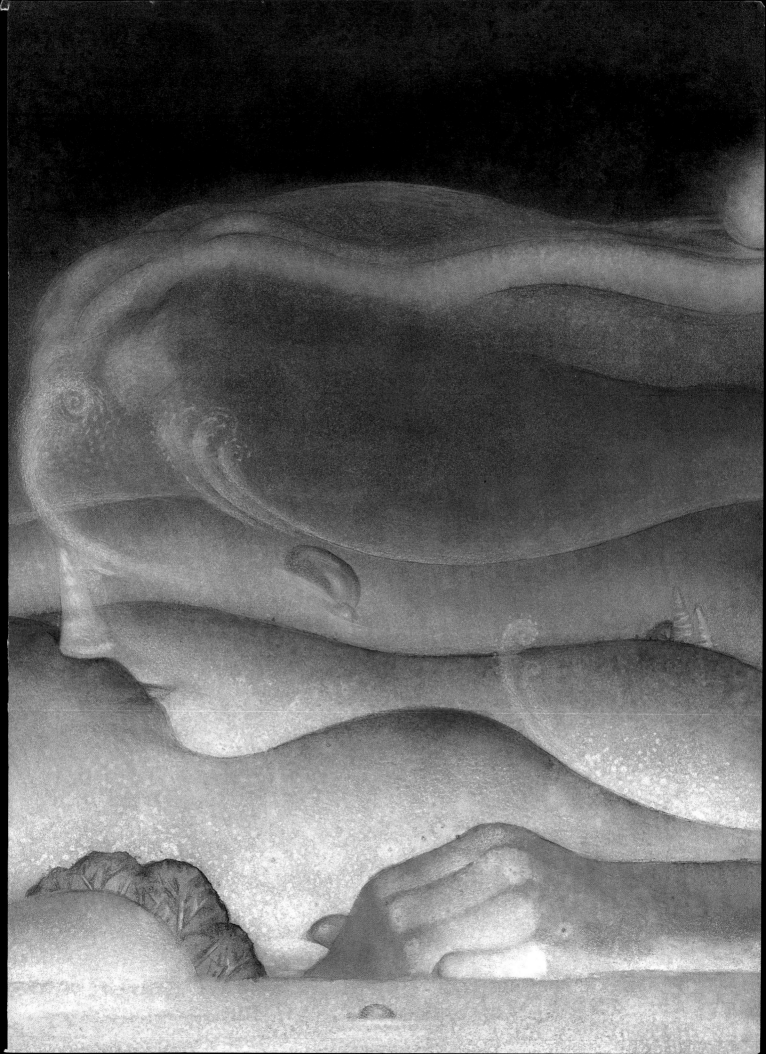

But her eyes opened wide,
as before her she spied
another child stirring,
a-swooshing, a-swirling,
bouncing on the bed.
"Can't sleep," Winter said.